The Little Red Hen

and other
Folk Tales

Retold by Starfall

The stories in this book can be read online with
interactive animation and sound at:

www.**starfall**.com

See the *"Folk Tales"* in the
"I'm Reading" section of the website.

ISBN: 978-1-59577-055-4

Starfall Education
P.O. Box 359, Boulder, Colorado 80306

Table of Contents

Foreword
For Parents and Teachers

Oral (spoken) language is thousands of years older than written language, and folk tales have been part of the oral tradition in every culture. This oral tradition makes use of repeated sentence patterns to enhance listeners' understanding of the story.

The Little Red Hen and Other Folk Tales is an anthology of delightful tales drawn from the literature of England, Russia, America, and the Far East. The stories are written with predictable, repetitive language patterns that encourage the participation of the young child. Emergent readers draw upon their own oral language and prior knowledge to anticipate each story's development. Young children enjoy predicting what will happen next in a story. Repetitive text develops their self-confidence and improves their reading fluency.

Research conducted in the United States, Great Britain, and Russia has demonstrated that exposing children to word and structure repetition through patterned books leads to automaticity and reading fluency. The National Reading Panel reviewed decades of reading research and concluded that fluency is one of the five foundational pillars of reading. That is why these tales are perfect for the beginning reader.

The stories in this collection have charming characters and settings, engaging plots, and implicit but clear themes. The characters and settings are elucidated through the clever use of captivating illustrations. Each plot develops sequentially. The central theme in each story in *The Little Red Hen and Other Folk Tales* is a universal truth such as those expressed in proverbs from around the world.

The stories in this collection will stimulate a discussion of universal moral themes that can be related to children's own lives as they encounter similar situations, personally or vicariously, throughout their formative years.

Dale D. Johnson, Ph.D.
Professor of Literacy Education
Dowling College, New York
Past President, International
Reading Association

Bonnie Johnson, Ph.D.
Professor of Human
Development and Learning
Dowling College, New York

Introduction

Children around the world love to hear folk tales, and parents and grandparents love to tell them. Folk tales are very old stories that have been passed down from great-grandparents to grandparents, from grandparents to parents, and from parents to children, for hundreds of years!

People keep telling these stories year after year because they help us learn about ourselves. As you read, think about the story. It might make you think about your own life.

Try this: After reading the English folk tale "The Little Red Hen," ask yourself, "What would I have done if I were the Little Red Hen? Would I have shared with my friends even if they hadn't helped me?" Talk about your ideas with your friends, parents, or teacher. Always respect each person's point of view. Remember, there are no right or wrong answers.

The folk tales in this book come from many countries. When you read them, you will learn about traditions and cultures that may be different from your own. It can be fun to compare two folk tales. You can think about the ways they are the same, and the ways they are different from each other.

Try this: Read the Far Eastern folk tale "The Four Friends." In this story, four completely different characters work together as a team and they all benefit. Now, compare this story with "The Little Red Hen," where the characters do not work together and no one benefits.

When you think and talk about the things you read, you will discover that books contain all kinds of ideas. These ideas can help you learn about yourself, other books that you've read, and the world you live in!

Have fun reading!
The Starfall Team

Editor's Notes on Folk Tales

We selected the stories in this collection to represent the familiar and the exotic, the very old and the brand new; in short, to encapsulate the best qualities of the folk tale genre. Tied to oral language, folk tales readily bend, evolve, and are born to suit their times and audiences.

Some of the folk tales in this book have been edited for brevity or content. "The Little Red Hen" traditionally begins with the hen discovering wheat, followed by any combination of the following: planting, harvesting, milling, carrying, mixing, and baking bread. Our telling of "The Little Red Hen" substitutes corn for wheat, but the theme is unchanged: If you are unwilling to help out with the work, please don't expect to enjoy the rewards. Traditionally, the foolish birds in "Chicken Little" are eaten by Foxy Loxy. In our version, Foxy Loxy wisely scolds the birds. We feel that this is a much nicer way to teach a lesson!

Bhutan is a far-eastern country located in the Himalayan Mountains north of India. "The Four Friends" is one of this country's favorite folk tales. In fact, paintings of a peacock, rabbit, monkey, and elephant standing one on top of the other is a common appearance in many buildings and homes there. This story demonstrates the value of working together for the benefit of all.

"The Turnip" is a famous Russian folk tale. It helps us see that even the smallest person (or mouse!) can make an important contribution towards reaching a common goal.

"The Little Rooster" is based on a story attributed to 19th century American author Charles Loomis. The events in this tale remind us of Benjamin Franklin's advice: Early to bed and early to rise makes a man healthy, wealthy, and wise.

"Mr. Bunny's Carrot Soup" is a modern folk tale written by American author Jennifer Greene. It teaches us the unexpected rewards that can come from selfless giving. Only time will tell if her story will become a traditional favorite like the others in this book. You can help by reading it and passing it on!

The Little Red Hen

An English Folk Tale

A little red hen found a bag of corn. "I will take it home and make muffins," she said.

The little red hen asked a duck, "Will you please help me lift my bag of corn?"

The duck said, "No."

She asked a turkey, "Will
you please help me lift
my bag of corn?"

The turkey said, "No."

She asked a goose, "Will you please help me lift my bag of corn?"

The goose said, "No."

"Then I will lift it myself!" said the little red hen.

The little red hen tried to make muffins.

"I will ask for help," she said.

The little red hen asked the duck, "Will you please help me make muffins?"

The duck said, "No."

She asked the turkey,
"Will you please help me
make muffins?"

The turkey said, "No."

She asked the goose,
"Will you please help me
make muffins?"

The goose said, "No."

"Then I will make them myself,"
said the little red hen.

The duck, the turkey, and
the goose went to the little
red hen's house.

"The muffins smell yummy!"
they said. "Can we help you
eat them?"

"No," said the little red hen.

"You did not help me lift
the bag. You did not help
me make the muffins. So I
will not share my muffins
with you."

Chicken Little
(The Sky Is Falling)
An English Folk Tale

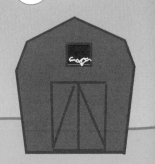

One day, a leaf landed on Chicken Little's tail.

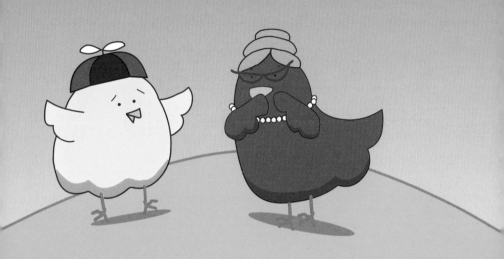

He ran to Henny Penny
and cried, "The sky is
falling!"

"Oh! I must tell everyone!"
cried Henny Penny.

Soon Henny Penny met
Ducky Lucky.

"The sky is falling!"
cried Henny Penny.

Ducky Lucky asked, "How
do you know that?"

"Chicken Little told me,"
said Henny Penny.

"We must tell everyone!"
cried Ducky Lucky.

Soon they met
Goosey Loosey.

"The sky is falling!"
cried Ducky Lucky.

Goosey Loosey asked,
"How do you know that?"

"Henny Penny told me,"
cried Ducky Lucky.

"Chicken Little told me,"
cried Henny Penny.

"We must tell everyone!"
cried Goosey Loosey.

Soon they met
Turkey Lurkey.

"The sky is falling!"
cried Goosey Loosey.

Turkey Lurkey asked,
"How do you know that?"

"Ducky Lucky told me,"
cried Goosey Loosey.

"Henny Penny told me,"
cried Ducky Lucky.

"Chicken Little told me,"
cried Henny Penny.

"We must tell everyone!"
cried Turkey Lurkey.

Soon they met Foxy Loxy.

"The sky is falling!"
cried Turkey Lurkey.

Foxy Loxy asked, "How
do you know that?"

"Goosey Loosey told me,"
cried Turkey Lurkey.

"Ducky Lucky told me,"
cried Goosey Loosey.

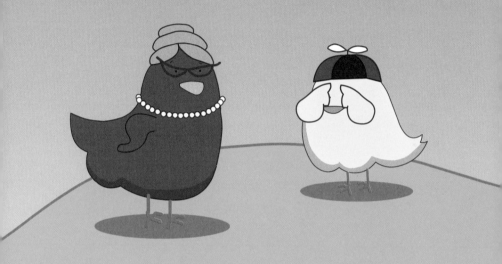

"Henny Penny told me,"
cried Ducky Lucky.

"Chicken Little told me,"
cried Henny Penny.

"Look!" said Foxy Loxy.
"Do you *see* the sky falling?"

"No, we don't see it falling,"
   they said.

"Listen!" said Foxy Loxy.
"Do you *hear* the sky falling?"

"No, we don't hear it falling,"
they said.

"Feel!" said Foxy Loxy.
"Do you *feel* the sky falling?"

"No, we don't feel it falling,"
  they said.

"Silly birds," said Foxy Loxy.
"Next time, see, hear, and feel
for yourselves before you tell
everyone else!"

Mr. Bunny's Carrot Soup

A Modern American Folk Tale
by Jennifer Greene

Mr. Bunny picked four carrots.

"I will make carrot soup," he said.

Then he met Mr. Rat.

Mr. Rat asked, "May I have a carrot, please?"

"Yes, take one," said Mr. Bunny.

"Thank you," said Mr. Rat.

Mr. Bunny had three carrots left.

Then he met Miss Pig.

Miss Pig asked, "May I have a carrot, please?"

"Yes, take one," said Mr. Bunny.

"Thank you," said Miss Pig.

Mr. Bunny had two carrots left.

Then he met Mr. Duck.

Mr. Duck asked, "May I have a carrot, please?"

"Yes, take one," said Mr. Bunny.

"Thank you," said Mr. Duck.

Mr. Bunny had one carrot left.

Then he met Miss Hen.

Miss Hen asked, "May I have a carrot, please?"

"Yes, take the last one," said Mr. Bunny.

"Thank you," said Miss Hen.

Mr. Bunny went home
without any carrots.

"Now I can't make my carrot
soup!" he said.

Then the doorbell rang:
ding-dong, ding-dong!

"Who is it?" asked Mr. Bunny.

"Hello!" said Mr. Rat, Miss
    Pig, Mr. Duck, and Miss Hen.

"Why are you all here?" asked
    Mr. Bunny.

"You shared your carrots
with us," they said, "so we
will share our food with you."

"Thank you," said Mr. Bunny.
"What did you make?"

"We made carrot soup!" they
said. "Let's eat!"

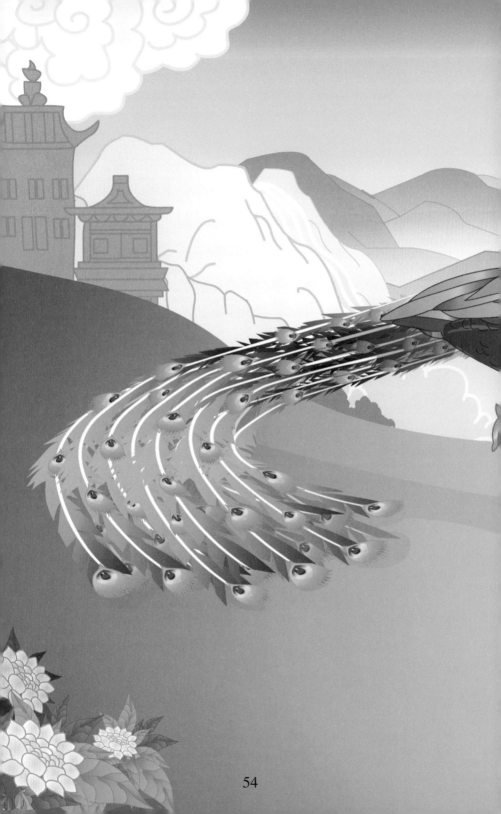

The Four Friends

A Tale from the Far East

One day, a peacock
planted a little seed.

Along came a rabbit.
She asked, "Can I help?"

"Yes," said the peacock.
"Please water the seed."

So the rabbit watered
the seed.

Along came a monkey.

He asked, "Can I help?"

"Yes," said the rabbit.
"Please feed the seed."

So the monkey fed the seed.

Along came an elephant.

She asked, "Can I help?"

"Yes," said the monkey.
"Please watch the seed."

So the elephant watched
the seed.

The little seed grew
into a little plant.

The little plant grew
into a big tree.

Big red apples grew on
the tree!

"I cannot reach the apples!"
cried the elephant.

"I can help!" said the monkey.

He jumped onto the
elephant's back.

"I cannot reach the apples!"
cried the monkey.

"I can help!" said the rabbit.

She jumped onto the
monkey's back.

"I cannot reach the apples!" cried the rabbit.

"I can help!" said the peacock.

He jumped onto the rabbit's back.

"Now I can reach them!" said the peacock.

The four friends had
worked together.

Now they had yummy
apples to eat.

The
Little
Rooster

An American Folk Tale

Once there was a farmer who had a little rooster.

At night he put it in the hen yard.

"I am so tired!" he told the rooster. "Let me sleep late tomorrow morning."

The little rooster woke up with the sun.

He jumped out of the yard and ran to the house.

He flapped his wings and cried,
"Cock-a-doodle-doo!"

The farmer woke up and yelled, "Go away!"

The rooster ran back to the yard.

The farmer said, "Now
that I am up, I will plant
my garden."

That night the farmer put the little rooster into a pigpen.

"I am so tired!" he told the rooster. "Let me sleep late tomorrow morning."

The little rooster woke up with the sun.

He jumped out of the pigpen.
He ran to the house.

He flapped his wings and
cried, "Cock-a-doodle-doo!"

The farmer woke up and
yelled, "Go away!"

The rooster ran back to
the pen.

The farmer said, "Now
that I am up, I will weed
my garden."

That night he put the little rooster into the barn.

"I am so tired!" he told the rooster. "Let me sleep late tomorrow morning."

The little rooster woke up with the sun.

He jumped out of the barn.
He ran to the house.

He flapped his wings and cried,
"Cock-a-doodle-doo!"

The farmer woke up, picked up the little rooster, and gave it away.

That night the farmer told himself, "I will sleep late tomorrow morning."

The farmer did sleep late

the next morning,

and the next,

and the next.

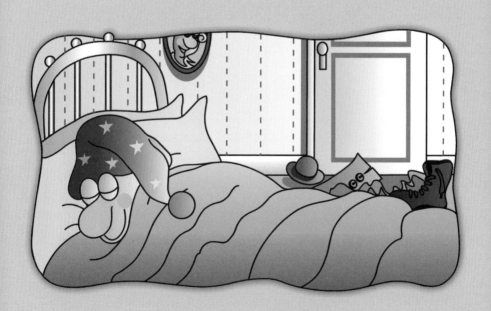

He became very lazy without the little rooster to wake him.

Now his garden is full of weeds!

The Turnip

A Russian Folk Tale

A farmer planted a turnip.
It got bigger,
and bigger,
and bigger.

One day the farmer said,
"I am going to pull up that
big turnip."

He pulled and pulled, but the
turnip did not come up.

The farmer called his wife.
"Please help me!" he cried.
"Hold on to me. Pull when
I pull."

The farmer pulled on the turnip.
The wife pulled the farmer.

They pulled and pulled, but
the turnip did not come up.

The wife called her child.
"Please help us!" she cried.
"Hold on to me. Pull when
I pull."

The farmer pulled on the turnip.
The wife pulled the farmer. The
child pulled the wife.

They pulled and pulled, but
the turnip did not come up.

The child called a dog.
"Please help us!" she cried.
"Hold on to me. Pull when
I pull."

The farmer pulled on the turnip.
The wife pulled the farmer.
The child pulled the wife.
The dog pulled the child.

They pulled and pulled, but
the turnip did not come up.

The dog called a cat.
"Please help us!" he cried.
"Hold on to me. Pull when
I pull."

the turnup

The farmer pulled on the turnip.
The wife pulled the farmer.
The child pulled the wife.
The dog pulled the child.
The cat pulled the dog.

They pulled and pulled, but
the turnip did not come up.

The cat called a mouse.
"Please help us!" she cried.
"Hold on to me. Pull when
   I pull."

The farmer pulled on the turnip.

The wife pulled the farmer.

The child pulled the wife.

The dog pulled the child.

The cat pulled the dog.

The mouse pulled the cat.

They pulled, and pulled, and...

Pop! The turnip came up!

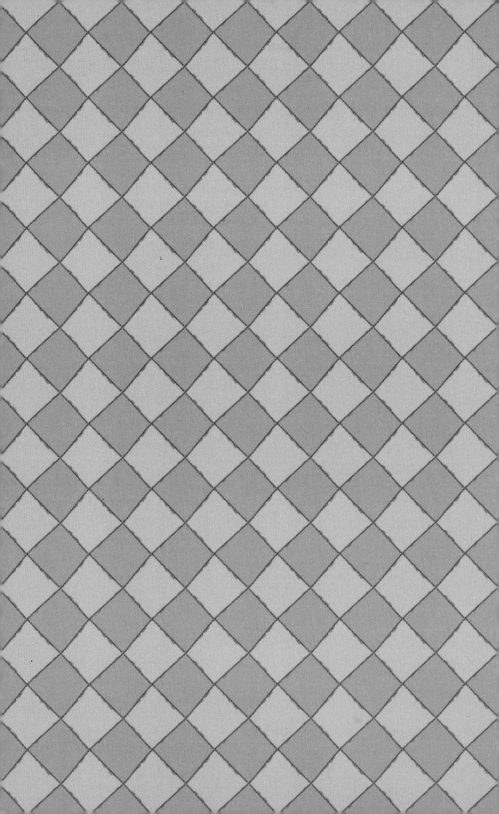